Impossible Encounters

Zoran Živković

Impossible Encounters
Copyright © 2000 by Zoran Živković

This edition copyright © 2019 Cadmus Press. All rights reserved. No part of this publication may be reproduced in whole or in part, or stored in a retrieval system, or transmitted in any form or by any means, electronic, mechanical, photocopying, recording, or otherwise, without written permission from the publisher.

FG-RS0013L
ISBN: 978-4-908793-12-7

Cover: Youchan Ito, Togoru Art Works

Neoclassic Fleurons font used with permission of
Paulo W–Intellecta Design

Cadmus Press
cadmusmedia.org

Impossible Encounters

Zoran Živković

Translated from the Serbian
by
Alice Copple-Tošić

Cadmus Press
2019

Contents

1. The Window   1
2. The Cone   15
3. The Bookshop   23
4. The Train   41
5. The Confessional   51
6. The Atelier   63

About the author   76
About the artist   78

1. The Window

I died in my sleep.

There wasn't anything special about my death. I hardly even noticed it. I dreamed I was walking down a long hallway closely lined with doors on both sides. The end of the corridor was invisible in the distance, and I was alone. On the wall next to each door hung a framed portrait, slightly larger than life, and lit from above by a lamp.

I looked at the paintings as I passed by them. What else could I do? Only the portraits disturbed the endless monotony of the corridor. There seemed to be male and female portraits in approximately equal numbers, but randomly distributed. The people were mostly of advanced age, and some were very old indeed, but here and there was a younger face, or even a child, though these were quite rare. The images were formal studio-portraits, and the people were all elaborately, even ceremonially dressed. They looked conscious of their own importance, and that of the occasion. Most of them were smiling, but some faces were simply not suited to smiling. They looked grimly serious.

I was not overly surprised when I finally saw my own portrait next to one of the doors. I hadn't actually expected it, but it didn't seem out of place. After all, if so many others had their portraits hanging there, why shouldn't I? Where else can one hope for a privileged position if not in one's own dream? The only thing that momentarily confused me was that I could not remember when the portrait had been painted. I must have posed for it, I supposed. But maybe that hadn't been necessary. It's hard to say. I don't pretend to understand much about portrait-painting.

Regardless of its origin, I liked the portrait. It did me full justice—more, it showed me in exceptionally good form. Although I was depicted at my current age, the painter had skillfully diminished some of the more unpleasant aspects of aging: he had slightly smoothed the wrinkles on my forehead and around my eyes, tightened my double chin, removed the yellowness and blotches from my cheeks, darkened some of the gray streaks in my hair. This was not to make me look younger. The years were still on the painting, but I bore them with greater elan. And most important of all, there was no sign of the debilitating disease that had taken such a heavy toll on my looks. No effort on the part of a photographer could ever have produced the same effect, however great his skill.

I stood in front of my portrait for a long time, gazing in satisfaction. But all things have their measure, even vanity. I couldn't stand there forever. Someone might pass by sooner or later and find me in this unbecoming position, which would certainly be embarrassing. But where could I go? Continue down the corridor? That did not seem promising; it appeared to extend endlessly before me, with no destination to make for.

Should I go back? That possibility hadn't crossed my mind before. I turned around and immediately understood I could not count on going back. Just a few steps behind me the hallway disappeared, turning into deep darkness, as though all the lamps above the paintings had turned off as soon as I passed them. Maybe the lights would go on again if I headed in that direction, but I had no desire to find out.

I turned to face forward again—and suffered a new

The Window

surprise. The same thing had happened to the corridor in front of me. It had turned into a dark tunnel that began at the edge of the small, conical beam of light illuminating my portrait from above. This sole remaining source of light covered the painting, the door beside it and myself in front of it—a tiny island of existence bounded by an opaque, black sea of nothingness.

I had lost the right to choose; there was only one path before me. The moment I touched the doorknob, I was overcome by the feeling that something important was about to happen, but I had no immediate inkling what it could be. It was only after I opened the door and entered the room that I realized I had died. It happened in the middle of raising and lowering my foot as I crossed the threshold. I was still alive when I started the step outside, and already dead when I finished it inside. I barely felt the transition itself. Something streamed through me, a wave resembling a light trembling or momentary shiver. It lasted a split second, then passed, leaving behind no other trace than the certainty of death.

I was not afraid. Fear of death has meaning before one dies, and not afterward. The only thing I felt was confusion. I naturally knew nothing about this state. How could I, after all? I had not even tried to picture it in my mind. That had always seemed a pointless exercise to me, and as the disease got the upper hand, such thoughts had come to fill me with revulsion—to be avoided as much as possible.

First of all, I wondered if I was still asleep. It is said that the deceased rest in eternal peace, but that is probably a metaphor, not meant be taken literally. In any case, the sight before me did not resemble in the least any that I had seen in my dreams. There was nothing unreal or strange. On the contrary. The room I entered was some sort of study, elegantly furnished to be sure, but otherwise not the least bit unusual. There was no one inside. Feeling a bit uncomfortable, I started to inspect it, without stepping away from the door, which I had closed behind me.

To my right stood a large, black, wooden desk. A lamp with an arching neck and green shade illuminated numerous objects, arranged in orderly fashion upon it: a wide, leather-bound desk-pad; a decorative brass inkwell with a heavy maple-wood blotter; a rosewood cube, drilled with holes to make a pen and pencil holder; a shallow lacquer paper tray; an ivory-handled magnifying glass; a double silver candlestick (without any candles); three identical little boxes covered in dark velour whose purpose I could not make out; a white flowerpot containing a flowerless plant with long, thin leaves; an engraved pipe stand with three pipes of different shapes.

Across from the desk, on the left-hand side, were two large brown leather armchairs with a small round coffee table between them. On the table was a lamp with a tasseled yellow shade, a book and an oval tray containing a lidded jug of water and two glasses placed upside down on round paper coasters. Behind the armchairs rose a bookshelf that covered the entire wall. The books in it were of uniform height and thickness, and their spines were bound in a limited range of somber tones. A vertical ladder rose along the edge of the bookshelf, its ends firmly anchored to guide-rails on the floor and ceiling.

The middle of the wall facing the door was covered by a large painting in a simple rectangular frame, positioned longside up, and brightly illuminated from below. It depicted an area of clear blue sky seen through a double window. The deep blue was portrayed so convincingly that for a moment I even took it for a real window.

The window was closed, but there was a certain tension in the otherwise tranquil scene that indicated it might open at any moment—through a draft, perhaps, or by someone going up to open it, someone who was

The Window

still not visible, but whose presence was hinted at by a shadow that flickered just inside the frame. The only thing that disturbed the harmony of the straight lines and uniform shades was a colorful butterfly that had already tired of its efforts to fly outside, clearly unable to understand the existence of a completely invisible, but still impenetrable obstacle such as glass.

To the right of the picture, in the semidarkness, stood a grandfather clock in a tall mahogany case. The glass door was decorated with geometric designs in the corners, and a disproportionately small key protruded from the keyhole. At first I thought I saw only one hand pointing straight up, but when I took a better look I discerned the small hand hidden under the big one. I stared at them for some time, but when they failed to change position I lowered my eyes suspiciously; only then did I notice that the pendulum was resting in the middle, motionless.

To the left of the painting, hard by the bookshelf, was another door. It was the same color as the wall around it and could only be distinguished by its edges, which appeared somewhat darker. It had an unusual characteristic that I did not notice at first glance. There was a lock, but no doorknob. If the door could be opened, then it was only possible from the other side.

Just as I was looking at it, that happened, quite soundlessly. Part of the wall seemed simply to arch forward, and a figure appeared in the emptiness left behind. I stared at it fixedly. Had I not been dead, I am sure that my heart would have jumped, and pins and needles would have run up and down my spine.

The man who appeared in front of me seemed unassuming, almost like a clerk: in late middle age, not very tall, balding, with a thick, narrow mustache that covered only the line under his nose, small, round, wire-rimmed glasses, and a dark suit of classic cut that did not quite succeed in hiding his extra pounds. The smile that appeared on his round, ruddy face seemed guileless and unaffected.

He hastened brightly to greet me, his hand stretched out. I had no recourse but to accept it.

"Welcome! Welcome!"

I didn't know what to say in return, so I smiled too, although mine was somewhat forced. We stood there like that for some time, gripping each other's hands, eyeing each other curiously, like friends meeting after a long separation.

He was the first to break the silence. "Please, make yourself comfortable." He indicated one of the armchairs in front of the bookshelf, waited for me to sit down, and then sat down in the other, hitching up his trouser legs a bit. He was still smiling.

"I was expecting you earlier. You stayed a bit longer than planned."

His voice seemed to contain a touch of reproach, but that might have been my imagination. He looked at me in silence for several moments, perhaps expecting me to say something. As I remained silent, he waved his hand at last, dismissively.

"Well, it's all the same. Some are late, some are early. There are very few who arrive on time. They all come, however, sooner or later. How do you feel?"

I cleared my throat before answering uncertainly. "Fine, I think."

He nodded his head in satisfaction. "Nothing is bothering you, there is no discomfort?"

I paused briefly. "No, everything's all right."

The man's smile broadened. "I'm glad to hear that. You're just a bit confused, yes?"

"Yes," I admitted after a moment's hesitation, "a little."

"You mustn't reproach yourself for that. You're no exception in this regard. They're all confused when they arrive. It's quite normal. Would you like a glass of water?" He indicated the jug on the table between us.

The Window

"No, thank you," I replied. I had the ghostly impression that my throat was dry, but somehow it didn't seem appropriate to drink water in this new position. Maybe later, when I was used to it.

"People are really quite full of questions," continued the man. "They are dying of curiosity. I'm sure that you are, too."

There was no reason to pretend. "I hope that's normal, too."

"Of course, of course. You are certainly interested in where you have arrived, what awaits you here, and who I am, as well."

"Certainly," I agreed in a faltering voice.

"There is a little difficulty in this connection. I, naturally, can answer all these questions. And many others that you might like to ask. But if I do that, I will deprive you of the possibility of going back."

"Going back?"

"Yes. You can return. To life."

I stared fixedly at the stranger in the other armchair. His tiny eyes returned my glance good-naturedly through his round glasses.

"But I'm dead," I said finally, in a half-questioning voice.

"Yes, that's clear. Otherwise you wouldn't be here."

"Well, then, how . . ."

"I can't explain it to you. Unless you decide to stay."

Now my throat felt not only dry, but tight. I tried to swallow, without success. As I poured water from the jug into one of the glasses, my hand trembled a bit. I hoped this clumsiness had not been too conspicuous. The water was cold, but it tasted a little stale.

"Do you mean to say I'm the one who decides—whether I go back or stay?"

"You, of course. Who else?"

"I mean, it doesn't depend on my behavior in . . . my previous life? I might be someone really bad, for example."

The man gave a short laugh. "Yes, you might. But it

makes no difference. There is no punishment or reward here. This is not the Last Judgment."

"So, it's enough for me to decide to go back. Do I understand that correctly?"

"You understand correctly. You can even choose the shape in which you will return."

I put the glass back on the coaster. Small puddles of water that had spilled from the jug sparkled in the yellow light on the silver surface of the tray. Several drops had even fallen on the book nearby. Had it not been for that, I probably would not have paid attention to the illustration on the front cover. It was a reproduction of the painting of the window on the wall next to us, and above it was the title written in slender, yellow letters—*Impossible Encounters*. I was not familiar with the author's name.

"I wouldn't change my shape," I said. "I'm used to this one."

The smile disappeared from the man's lips. "I'm afraid that's the only thing that's impossible. Your old shape has been used up, it is no longer serviceable. You can't go back to it. And it would not be wise. Disease has completely destroyed you, isn't that so? But you can choose something completely new. The choice is almost unlimited."

"Be someone else?"

"You would not be someone else, because you would have no memory of your earlier life. It would be a new beginning for you."

"I would be born again?"

"Most assuredly. You would return to the world as a newborn child, as is fitting. To live a new life. With the characteristics that you want."

"You mean, I can choose what I'll look like, or how tall I'll be?"

"And much more than that. You could change the color of your skin, your sex . . ."

The Window

"Sex?"

The look of amazement that appeared on my face caused the stranger to smile once again. "That is one of the most frequent changes. In both directions. I think it's not so much dissatisfaction with one's original sex as much as curiosity about trying the opposite sex."

I shook my head. "Well, I'm not curious."

"I understand. Would you perhaps be interested in going back as something other than a human being? That is also possible."

I squinted my eyes in disbelief. "What do you mean?"

"There are other forms of life on earth besides humans. There are countless numbers, in fact. They are all at your disposal."

"What, for example?"

"Oh, anything. Of course, it all depends on the inclinations of the one going back. People usually choose an animal."

I paused slightly before answering. "Why would someone want to be an animal, and not a human, in his new life?"

"Well, it doesn't have to be at all as bad as you might think. The life of a pure-bred cat or thoroughbred horse, for example, could be much more comfortable and carefree than many human lives. And if you prefer excitement, there are few human experiences that can compare to what a lion, an eagle or a shark experiences every day."

I thought it over briefly. "I still don't think I want to be an animal."

"Whatever you want. There are other possibilities as well. You could be a plant."

"A plant?"

"Yes, that is not such a rare choice."

"But plants don't have any . . . any consciousness."

"That's true, but this drawback is compensated by

other advantages. A long life, for example. Almost every type of tree lives considerably longer than a man. Sequoias are highly valued in this regard. They are protected, which makes them additionally attractive. But even short-lived flowers have their admirers. People sometimes decide to go back as an orchid or a rose-blossom, even though they know they will only live one short season."

"But that's absurd. Getting the chance for a new life and wasting it on some flower . . ."

"They don't look at it like that. Beauty means everything to them. That is something we must accept. But there are some decisions that are truly hard to understand. Even for me. What would you say to going back as a salamander, a worm, as a sagebrush, a stinging-nettle or a spider?"

"A spider?" I repeated. My face twisted into a disgusted grimace.

"Yes, quite unpleasant, wouldn't you say?"

"I would not change at all," I rushed to say, shaking my head. "I would like to stay as similar as I could to myself in my previous life. If that's possible."

"Of course it is. The great majority choose just that. So this means you have decided to go back?"

I did not answer at once. A multitude of confusing questions swarmed inside me. Finally, one outweighed all the others. "If I returned, I would live out another lifetime, right?"

"Yes."

"And in the end I would die again?"

"That is inevitable, unfortunately."

"After that would I . . . come back here again?"

"No, you only come here once. After your second life all that remains is death. You are given no further choice."

He said this in an even voice, as though it were quite banal. I looked at him for a few moments without speaking.

The Window

"But what is this choice all about, anyway? On one side there is a new life. I understand that. But what's on the other side? What am I supposed to choose between?"

The stranger removed his glasses, took a large white handkerchief from the inside pocket of his jacket and started to wipe them. He did so patiently and with extreme care, and in the end lifted them against the table lamp to check them. Without them his face seemed somehow bare. He put them back on slowly, pressing them onto the bridge of his nose.

"They rarely get around to that question," he said at last. "Almost all of them immediately grab the chance to return. They're not interested in anything else."

"What do you say to the others?"

"Nothing specific. The most I can do is give them a hint. Anything more than that would endanger their return, if they decided to go back after all."

"A hint?"

"Yes," replied the man. "Please come with me."

He got up, waited for me to do the same, and then took me cordially by the arm and led me. At first I thought we were heading for the door through which he had entered, but we stopped in front of the large picture in the middle of the wall.

His voice dropped almost to a whisper. "Look at it carefully."

My eyes were filled with the sight of the blue heavens seen through the closed window. The moments passed by slowly. Nothing happened. When the change finally occurred, it first affected my sense of hearing and not my sight. Suddenly, as though from a great distance, I started to hear an even, steady drumming. I didn't recognize it at first. It was only when it grew louder in the surrounding silence that I realized it was the dull ticking of the clock. I did not need to turn my eyes towards the large mahogany case in the right-hand corner to know that the pendulum was no longer motionless.

As though in answer to this awakening sound, the picture came to life. The butterfly fluttered once, sluggishly, without hope of finally breaking out, and slid down a bit lower. The shadow moved because the hand outside the frame moved. The hand entered the frame and made for the middle of the window. It tried to beat its own shadow, but they reached the handle at the same time and turned it.

The moment the window opened, I was almost stunned by a rush of dizziness. The man's firm clasp on my arm was a welcome support without which I would have lost my balance and fallen. But the butterfly had no one to help it. The gust of wind easily whisked it off the smooth glass surface and sent it rushing into the blue infinity.

That very instant everything disappeared: the picture frame, the wall, the stranger, the entire study. I was in the middle of nothing and started to fall. I knew that I had to move my wings, that I was supposed to fly and not descend headlong, but I suddenly no longer knew how. Many flashes of an eternity filled with icy horror passed before I once again mastered this simple, instinctive skill. First my descent slowed down, then stopped, and when I finally started to climb on an ascending stream of air, I didn't have to move my wings at all. I just kept them spread out like two enormous, colorful twin sails in the middle of the vast open sea of air that surrounded me.

Fear turned into the rapture that always accompanies flying. I could have stayed there forever, surrendering to this tide of joy. Then, at an unspecified distance ahead of me, I caught sight of something wrinkled on the uniform fabric of blue. Something had started to thin the air, to dissolve it, something that appeared from underneath. It was bright, radiant, inviting. I flapped my wings energetically, wrenching myself away from the main airstream. The call that drew me, the

The Window

radiance coming from the other side of the firmament, was irresistible: the flame of a candle attracting a moth in the dark.

But I was not allowed to reach the light. The airstream suddenly changed direction. I tried to resist it feverishly, realizing in despair that I was being borne away from where I longed to go. The strength of my wings, however, was nothing compared to that powerful pull. I rushed backwards faster and faster, filled with a painful feeling of futility and helplessness. The window slammed shut after me when I flew back in, and the same moment I was swallowed up in darkness.

The darkness was not completely empty; it was filled with the beating of a colossal heart. It was a regular, uniform sound, but somehow I knew it would soon stop. That happened all at once, without any premonitory slowing. Dropping to the lowest point, the pendulum did not continue on the other side; it stopped there, having nothing else to measure. In the silence it left behind, my sight slowly returned.

I was still standing in front of the picture, staring at it, although there was no longer anything moving in it. The butterfly was drooping in one of the corners again, and the shadow was patiently waiting for the unseen hand to move. Another hand slightly increased its pressure around my arm.

"This way. You'll feel more comfortable if you sit down again."

I wanted to tell him that everything was all right with me, but I staggered at the very first step and was grateful for the support he offered. When we were settled in the armchairs, he poured some more water from the jug into my glass. I wasn't thirsty, but I still took a long drink.

The man did not speak right away, just watched me with his customary grin. He was clearly giving me the chance to collect my wits. And I was grateful for that, too.

"An exceptional painting, wouldn't you agree?" he said at last.

"Yes," I agreed after a brief hesitation, a little hoarsely. "Exceptional."

We stopped talking once again. Just then a thought crossed my mind, one completely inappropriate to the decisive moment at hand. The other glass was still turned upside-down on the tray, unused. I wondered if it was there incidentally, just like the multitude of other objects in the room, or if the stranger sometimes drank a little water from it.

"So? Have you chosen?" There was no impatience in his voice, and I felt under no pressure. He could have asked me something quite trivial in the same tone.

"A butterfly," I replied softly. "I would like to be a butterfly, of course."

He looked at me wordlessly for several moments, and then gave a brief nod. "Of course." His smile grew broader. He motioned towards the door next to the painting. "After you."

I got up, a little unsteadily, and headed in that direction, but after a few steps I stopped, confused. The door had no handle on this side. How could I open it? I thought about turning around to ask the man. But that very instant I realized there was no need, for there was no longer any door in front of me.

2. The Cone

I DIDN'T COME OUT of the clouds until I was almost at the top of the Cone.

Although it was the middle of summer, Dark Mountain seemed buried in autumn. Down in the valley this was just an ordinary overcast day, probably muggy and humid, but here at an elevation of almost two thousand meters everything was clothed in a grayness that was less transparent than mist and somehow denser and more palpable. The sky literally touched the ground right here. The clouds were filled with minute drops, embryos of rain, that seemed to be moving in all directions, not just downward. If the temperature were to drop by just a few degrees, they would turn into crystals of snow. This actually happened now and then, though they always quickly reverted. During the summer on Dark Mountain you could go through all four seasons in one day.

In such weather it was not advisable to take long walks since you could easily lose your way. If they went out at all, people stayed close to the hotel, keeping to the asphalt paths where the lighting was on, even though it was just past noon. But I was not afraid of getting lost. I'd been coming to Dark Mountain for years, both summer and winter, and not a day would go by without a visit to the Cone. I was certain that I could find my way there even on a moonless night, though I'd never tried.

The Cone was a projection on the western slope,

about two and a half kilometers from the hotel. The view from its peak was almost as fascinating as the one from the topmost craggy crest of Dark Mountain, accessible only to fully equipped mountain climbers. Owing to the Cone's almost perfect shape, from which it derived its name, it seemed to be artificially planted there. As you approached, it didn't give the impression of being steep, but it was. The climb to the top thus required not only agility but considerable effort as well, even though the distance to be covered was less than one hundred and fifty meters.

These difficulties discouraged most of the hotel guests from visiting the Cone. On fine days they would walk to its foot, but only a rare few would decide to undertake the climb. In any case, the small, windy plateau at the top only had room for three or four people at most. When the weather was bad, like today's, I could count on having the Cone all to myself.

I came out of the cloud all of a sudden. I wasn't far from the top when it started to lighten. The grayness around me didn't thin or become more transparent, it just changed shade, turning a bright white. And then I suddenly rose above the foggy mass, squinting at the blinding radiance of the sun.

I stopped, still in cloud from the waist down, and waited for my eyes to adjust. Above me stretched the immeasurable, bright blue firmament, and as far as I could see below me was a motionless sea, its uniformity disturbed here and there by the islands of mountain peaks similar to the one I had just reached, forming a scattered archipelago in the sky. This panorama was worth all the trouble of the climb.

"Strange to find yourself above the clouds, isn't it?"

I started at the unexpected voice. I'd been so certain that I would be the only one at the top of the Cone that I hadn't even turned to look around, fixing my eyes on the horizon instead. The man was sitting on a rocky

The Cone

outcrop, his back turned to where I stood. It must have been the sound of my steps that told him I had joined him on the plateau. He was wearing a dark green jacket that blended in with the color of the surrounding grass and low bushes. His hair was gray and longish, partially covering his ears.

"It isn't usually crowded above the clouds," I replied, making little effort to hide my displeasure. I wasn't pleased at having to share the Cone with someone just then. I sat down on a patch of grass behind the stranger, feeling beforehand to see if it was wet. Among the thick tangle I found an empty can of soda pop carelessly left there. I picked it up and threw it into the depths below. I was aware that this was just as careless, but it seemed somehow more fitting for garbage to be found anywhere but here.

"No, it isn't. I liked it best when I could be alone here, too." He said this without any reproach in his voice, which made me feel awkward. In fact, he could consider me the intruder since he had reached the top of the Cone first. "But I won't bother you for long. I'll be leaving soon."

"You don't have to go because of me," I said obligingly. "There's room for both of us."

The man did not reply, so we fell silent, gazing into the distance. The warmth I started to feel wasn't just from the strenuous climb. It was considerably warmer here in the sun than down in the clouds. I did not unbutton my jacket, however, even though I could feel the sweat breaking out; the wind that never seemed to die down here at the top might blow through me.

"I haven't been on the Cone for a long time," said the man pensively, as though addressing someone invisible in front of him, rather than myself. "The last time I climbed up here I was your age."

I stared at his back in amazement. How could he

know my age when he hadn't turned around to look at me? Probably by my voice. I hadn't seen his face, either, but even without the gray hair I could easily tell by his hoarse, wheezing voice that he was well into his sixties.

"You've missed quite a bit," I said with a smile.

"I know. I'm trying to make up for it now. I'm visiting places that meant something to me in the past."

"Did you stay at Dark Mountain very often?"

"Yes, at least twice a year. I never did learn to ski, although I loved to take long walks."

"Me, too. I'm not the least bit bothered by not being able to ski. Walking is just as pleasant, and you need a lot less equipment."

The gray head nodded in front of me. "At first I went for walks in different directions. But after I discovered the Cone, I gave up all the other places. I started coming here every day, almost like a ritual. Over time it became a real obsession. The only thing that could stop me was a snowstorm."

Strange, I thought. It's as if the old man was describing my own experience. I never imagined I'd ever find such a kindred spirit. Most people think I'm an oddball because of my pilgrimages to the Cone. There was, however, one important difference.

"But it seems you got over your obsession. If I understood correctly, you stopped visiting the Cone. What prevented you from coming?"

The man did not reply at once. When he finally spoke again, his voice became softer, so that I had trouble making it out against the howling of the wind.

"I experienced something unusual here. Afterwards there was no sense in coming here any more."

I expected him to continue, but as the old man didn't elaborate, I had to curb my curiosity. For some reason he clearly did not want to talk about it, and good manners would not let me probe. We passed another few minutes in silence. I could feel the skin

The Cone

on my face start to prickle under the strong mountain sun. I should have brought some sun screen, although I hadn't actually expected the top of the Cone to be above the clouds.

"I like to return to places that mean something to me, too," I said at length, just to keep the conversation going. Although he had said he would be leaving soon, the old man continued to sit there, and it seemed silly not to talk while we shared this cramped space. "But it's never like it was the first time. The place might be the same, but the time is always different. That can't be helped, I'm afraid."

"Except if you return to some place at the original time," he said, his voice still low.

"In the past?" I asked with an inadvertent cry of disbelief.

The old man raised the collar of his jacket a little to protect himself from the strong wind that had just come up. Although quite blistering, the sun was deceptive. It would be easy to catch cold.

"Yes, in the past."

"Then it really would be just like the first time. Except it isn't possible. You can't go back into the past."

"Even so, if you were offered the chance to go back, which time in your life would you choose?"

My eyes began to skim over the endless landscape that surrounded me. Far to the east the sun had finally triumphed over the clouds and now wooded hills could be seen though the mist. By late afternoon it would clear up here, too, and Dark Mountain would return to summertime.

"I've never thought about that," I said. "I don't know, maybe some point in my childhood. I would probably like to see myself as a boy." I stopped for a moment, staring blankly at the gray shroud beneath me. "That would certainly be strange—to meet your own self."

The old man turned his head a bit towards me,

enough so that I could see his thick gray beard and sunglasses, but then he faced forward again.

"Why your childhood? Do you feel you were happier then than later in life?"

"It's hard to say," I replied after a brief hesitation. "Perhaps more innocent. There were happy moments later on, of course, but they lacked that early innocence. It seems to be more and more precious as time goes by. But what about you? Which time in your life would you go back to?"

The man shrugged his shoulders. "At my age childhood is already far away and faded. I think I would choose something closer, something I remember better. I was very happy when I came here to the Cone. Perhaps even innocent, in the sense in which you talk about your childhood, although it didn't seem like that at the time. In any case, I left innocence behind me forever on the Cone. I would be happy to meet myself again from that time."

I wiped the sweat off my brow with the back of my hand. "I bet the other one would be just as happy. Maybe even more so. It would be a very useful encounter for him. You could tell him first hand what awaits him in the future, what he should stay away from, what he should avoid."

"Oh, no, not at all," replied the man quickly, raising his voice a little. "I wouldn't tell him that at all."

"You wouldn't tell your own self what the future holds in store?"

"No."

"Why?"

"Because I would ruin my own life if I did. The encounter itself would be extremely risky. It would be best if he didn't realize who he'd met."

"I don't understand."

"If I told him what the future holds, I would be depriving him of the foundations that make life possible.

The Cone

Everything would become preordained for him, inevitable. He would lose not only hope but fear. And how can you live without hope or fear?"

"But what if, for example, there was some great misfortune or suffering awaiting him, that could easily be avoided if he was forewarned? Would you allow that to happen?"

"Of course."

"Wouldn't that be cruelty towards your own self?"

"Perhaps. But there is actually no choice. You cannot prevent what has already happened, can you?"

I didn't know what to reply. I had the vague feeling that there was some sort of paradox involved, but I couldn't put my finger on it. No doubt it all hung from the unfeasibility of the initial assumption about returning to the past.

The old man stood up and so did I. He was approximately my height, perhaps a bit stooped owing to the weight of his years. He picked up something he had been sitting on, and as he brushed off the bits of grass I realized it was a book. Before he put it in his pocket, I managed to read the large title—*Impossible Encounters*—but not the name of the writer.

He stayed a few moments more, staring at the sea of clouds that had now gently started to stir and thin out. Then he turned towards me and we were face to face for the first time.

I couldn't really see much of his face. It was hidden by his beard and the large sunglasses. Only his forehead was uncovered—it was even higher than mine because the gray strands had receded quite a bit towards the crown of his head.

"It's time to leave," he said. It might have been my imagination, but his voice seemed to tremble slightly, just like mine on the rare occasions when I am excited. He extended his hand and I took it in mine—a slim, bony hand, just like mine will probably be when

Impossible Encounters

I reach his age. "The Cone is all yours. Enjoy it while you can. One never knows what the future will bring."

"I'm glad we met," I said, more softly than I intended.

"I'm glad, too. Very glad."

He let go of my hand with some hesitation, almost unwillingly. Then he turned and headed down the steep slope, without looking back. He walked slowly, carefully. Like an old man. When he disappeared into the cloud, I felt a sudden lump in my throat.

I stayed on the Cone for a long time that day. Almost until dusk. By the middle of the afternoon everything below me had cleared up. I slowly absorbed the endless, luminous panorama surrounding me. I wanted to remember it well. I intended, of course, to come again next day, but the old man was right: I did not know what lay in store for me. What if something prevented me from coming? What if a long time, several decades, passed before I happened to climb the Cone again?

3. The Bookshop

THE FOG, AS USUAL, set in swiftly.

Only a few minutes had passed since the last time I'd raised my eyes from the computer screen and looked out of the bookshop's large display window. In the early twilight I had been able to see buildings on the other side of the river quite clearly, speckled with the first evening lights. Now everything had suddenly disappeared in the thick greyness; not only the opposite bank but also the long row of horse chestnut trees extending along the quay on this side of the river, just a few steps away. Although this transformation had taken place almost every evening since the middle of autumn, it never ceased to fascinate me. One moment the world was there, real, visible, tangible; then, in what seemed like the twinkling of an eye it would magically dissolve in the humid breath of the river spirits.

I could have closed the bookshop and gone home. For days no one had entered the shop after the fog rose. In autumn the river reversed its genial summer personality. When the weather was warm, the promenade under the horse chestnut trees was thronged till late in the evening. Then I would often stay open until midnight and sometimes even later, until the last customer had finally finished leafing through what I hoped would shortly be his book. The customer has always come first in this bookshop. But now I remained in the shop not only because the shop hours posted on the door obliged me to. I did not have a computer at home, and it seemed somehow inappropriate for me to write science fiction in the old-fashioned way, pen to paper.

But tonight I was not to be allowed to return my attention to the screen. My eyes were still gazing, unfocused, at the wall of mist on the other side of the window, when a figure took shape in front of the entrance, seeming to materialize out of nowhere. Its sudden appearance, unannounced by any footsteps on the pavement—unless, lost in thought, I had simply not heard them—made me start. Fog is apt to produce such eerie surprises, and I disliked it almost as much for that as for taking away my customers.

The man who came in was small and slight, with a short, sparse beard and wire-rimmed glasses. Although he appeared youthful, his grizzled sideburns and the silver streaks in his beard, particularly on his double chin, strongly suggested that he had passed the half-century mark. I have a good memory for faces, so one glance was enough to tell me that I had never seen him here before.

It must have been rather cold outside, for no sooner had the visitor entered the heated air of the bookshop than moisture condensed on his glasses, fogging them up completely. He stood by the door without moving, seeming to stare fixedly at me through large, empty eyes of unearthly blankness.

I pressed two keys at the same time, saving the text. This was not really necessary, as I had made no changes since the previous save, but that is what I always do, automatically, whenever there is about to be a break in work.

"Good evening," I said. "The fog is really thick tonight."

The man took off his glasses. He rummaged for a while through his long, green coat until he found a crumpled white handkerchief in an inside pocket and started to wipe his glasses. His movements were brisk and impatient, and left patches of condensation by the edges of the frame when he put them back on.

"This is a science fiction bookshop." It was somewhere between a question and a statement. There was something strange about the way he drew out his vowels, as if he were a foreigner who had learned the language well, but still hadn't quite mastered the proper accent.

"That's right," I replied with a smile, *"Polaris.* At your service. If it weren't for this terrible fog you wouldn't have to ask. There's a large neon sign above the entrance, but what good is it now? I paid a ton of money for it, but they forgot to tell me that it's completely useless in the fog. It would probably be better to turn it off. Drives customers away more than it attracts them. Even when you're right under it, it just looks like a bright, shiny rebus."

Still standing by the door, the visitor began to look around the shop. He slowly skimmed the shelves full of books and magazines, appearing somewhat bewildered, as though he had entered some amazing place, and not an ordinary bookshop at all. That is to say, maybe not exactly ordinary, since science fiction bookshops are a bit unusual, but they don't generally induce such bewilderment.

"I'm looking for a . . . work of science fiction," said the man, after his eyes had finally reached the counter with the cash register and computer, next to the display window, where I was sitting. His voice sounded hesitant, as though he had trouble choosing his words.

"Then you've come to the right address," I replied cordially. "We offer a wide selection of science fiction—new editions and secondhand. We really pride ourselves on them. We've got some truly old books. Real rarities you won't find anywhere else. And should we happen to be temporarily out of what you want, we can get it very quickly. In two or three days at most."

Impossible Encounters

The visitor finally moved away from the door and headed towards the counter. He stopped uncertainly when he got close to me, as though not knowing what to do with himself. I got a sudden whiff of a fresh, outdoorsy smell. It immediately brought to mind newly mown grass. The man must use a deodorant based on plant extracts.

"The work I'm looking for is in this bookshop," he said. His tone had lost its previous uncertainty and become self-confident. Even more than that: he said it in a voice that would brook no objection. "And it's not old at all. Quite the contrary, it's just been written."

"In that case," I replied, "it must be here." I got up from my chair and headed towards the shelf where I kept the latest editions. "Here you are."

Seven narrow rows contained some fifty books that had been published in the last several months. Science fiction was on the upswing again. This time last year those shelves had held barely fifteen volumes. I reached towards the middle shelf and pulled out a rather small book with a shiny cover.

"This is our most recent acquisition—*Impossible Encounters*. Might this be what you are looking for?"

The customer briefly examined the book in my hand, then shook his head. "No, that's not it."

"I suggest you have a look at the other books. These are all recent editions."

I left the visitor in front of the shelf and returned to the counter. People don't like you to hover round while they leaf through a book. It gives them an unpleasant feeling of being under surveillance.

My eyes dropped to the screen, with its tangle of words. The story I was writing was practically finished. All that was left was to read it once again and polish it up here and there. I would have had no trouble doing so in the solitude I'd expected until I closed the shop. Now that solitude had been interrupted, but I hoped the man would quickly find what he was looking for so that I could resume my concentration on the text. I could not, of course, work while he was there. Not knowing what else to do while I waited, I pushed the 'save' keys once more.

My fingers were still on the keyboard when the visitor came up to me again. At first I thought he'd found the book he wanted, but when I raised my eyes I saw that his hands were empty.

"It's not there," he said.

"You've already looked at everything?" I asked, unable to conceal a note of disbelief.

"Yes, there are only forty-eight books," he replied in an even tone. If he'd noticed the surprise in my voice, he did nothing to show it.

I gazed briefly at the man in front of me, and then at the shelf with new editions. "Why, yes," I said at last, "only forty-eight."

"Where else could I look?" he asked rather quickly.

"If it's a really new book, then that's the only place it could be. I don't keep them anywhere else. The other shelves contain older editions. Which book are you looking for? If you tell me the title, I can help you find it."

"Title?" The visitor squinted in dismay through his glasses, which were now dry. "I don't know the title."

"It doesn't matter," I hastened to assure him. This was by no means a rare occurrence. I encountered variously incomplete requests almost every day. "The writer's name will be enough. That will make it easy for us to find the book."

The man took his handkerchief out of his pocket once again and wiped the top of his forehead. He was clearly dressed too warmly for indoor temperatures, and beads of sweat had started to break out. I was assailed by another outdoor smell. Instead of mown grass it was some wildflower this time, but I couldn't determine which.

Impossible Encounters

"I don't know the author's name." A look of unease crossed his face.

I sighed inwardly. Any chance of finishing work on my story that evening was receding. This was likely to take some time.

"Why don't you make yourself more comfortable," I suggested. "It's rather warm in here, and it may take us a while to find this work, with its unknown title and unknown author. You can leave your coat on the hook by the door."

The visitor shook his head briskly. "No, no. I can't take off my coat. I don't have much time. It's an urgent matter. I have to find the work as soon as possible. I can't go back without it. You don't understand. . . ."

He said this very quickly, in one breath, and then suddenly stopped, as though for some reason he couldn't or didn't want to continue. A pleading look came into his eyes.

"I do understand," I replied after a short pause. "You want to find a specific work of science fiction and you are in a hurry. I certainly want to help you, but you have made only very scanty data available to me. All that I know is that it is some new work and that you didn't find it on the shelf over there. If you could tell me something more about it, I might recognize it. I read a lot, almost everything that comes out. Particularly new things. Could you at least give me some idea of what the work is about?"

A smile played on the man's lips. "That I can do, yes. Certainly. It is about my world."

We stood there several moments looking at each other without speaking. I was smiling too.

"Your world?" I repeated, breaking the silence first.

"Yes, but you on Earth know nothing about it. Or rather, nothing was known until recently. Until the work I am searching for was written. Our star doesn't even have a name here, just a number, although it is relatively close, less than eleven and a half light years away. But it's a small star, much less conspicuous than those around it, so there's nothing strange in it being anonymous."

I slowly nodded my head to indicate understanding, as if he were telling me something quite commonplace. So that was it. One more of those. Yet he hadn't the look of one. Quite the contrary. But appearances can be deceptive, as had been proved often enough. Clothes alone do not the eccentric make.

All kinds of oddballs visit my bookshop. They seem to be irresistibly drawn to it, and they constitute an ineluctable hazard of my chosen genre. I am most often visited by those who have had first-hand experience with extraterrestrials, and for some reason feel this is the right place to bare their souls. At first I entered into discussions with them, explaining that I class science fiction as imaginative prose. Their real-life experiences had no place in this category, for the very reason that they were real. As a rule, however, this distinction was too fine for them.

Then, in my naiveté and inexperience I tried to talk them out of it. Why go to the inconvenience and expense of shooting across from the other side of the cosmos, only to subject some commonplace citizen in an isolated house to unusual lights or sounds? That was when I got into serious trouble. Not only did they turn a deaf ear to the reasons I cited, they resolutely interpreted my unwillingness to believe them as reliable confirmation that I, too, was part of the great conspiracy to hush up visits by extraterrestrials. That was the milder version. Several flying saucer fans accused me openly and rather peevishly of being an extraterrestrial myself.

There is no complete defense against such accusations. Indeed, how can anyone prove he is not an extraterrestrial to someone who can see antennae sprouting from his forehead? What arguments can ever shake the believer's blind conviction? But to me the primary difficulty stemmed from my profession. As the owner of a bookshop I could hardly draw distinctions among my customers based on their view of the world, so my hands were tied. Should I meet this type of person in some other context, I could solve the problem simply by raising my voice. A slightly sharper tone has a truly amazing effect on them. They fall silent at once and withdraw, often in embarrassment. But here, that would be out of the question. How would it look if a bookshop-owner yelled at those customers who just happened to take a somewhat unusual view of his ancestry?

And so I resorted to the last means still at my disposal. Whenever an eccentric like this one drops in, I listen to his story with utmost patience, regardless of how far-fetched it is, taking great care to speak as little as possible. My most frequent reaction is to nod or shake my head from time to time, as befits the situation, to demonstrate that I am carefully following the story. This technique has often proved useful. First of all, the whole affair is concluded far more quickly than if one were to start a discussion; second, after baring his soul almost every single visitor of this kind ends up buying a book.

Over time this proved adequate compensation for approximately a quarter hour of my attention. I could almost have made this part of my price list: "The purchase of a book gives the buyer the right to squander fifteen minutes of the owner's time in any way he sees fit". At first my conscience bothered me a bit, feeling this partook of prostitution; then my business sense over-rode such improvident moral purism.

Furthermore, over time I came to see myself as a psychiatrist—a rather poorly paid psychiatrist, it's true, but at least there was never a shortage of patients. Quite the contrary. There were so many of them I could no longer rely on memory alone, and had had to buy a notebook in which to write down what each one of them bought, so they would not accidentally buy the same book twice. This, to be sure, didn't bother them in the least, since most of the books were never read—occasionally I even found them discarded next to a nearby trashcan—but for me this was a matter of professional attitude towards my work. Every customer deserves the best possible treatment, and the handicapped get a bonus to boot.

But never before had I encountered a case like this. This was the first time that an extraterrestrial had visited my bookshop! Perhaps I should have been jealous. Up till that moment the role had been reserved for myself. Granted, the situation hadn't changed essentially. It was just a matter of nuances. My basic strategy remained the same: don't question anything and encourage the speaker to tell his story without holding back.

"Eleven and a half light years," I said. "Why, that's really not so small. You had to travel quite a distance! It must have taken you a long time."

The man shook his head. "No time at all. It's hard even to call it travelling."

"I see. Did you spend the flight in hibernation, then? Is that why it seemed so short?"

"No, hibernation wasn't necessary."

"Oh. Then that means you must have a very fast spaceship. Judging by how quickly you got here, it must travel considerably faster than the speed of light."

He looked at me the way a teacher looks at a student who has blurted out an absurdity. "No spaceship can travel faster than the speed of light."

"Of course it can't," I said, hastening to correct myself. "How silly of me. I forgot that for a minute. Then how did you get here so fast? Excuse me for not being able to figure it out for myself—space travel is not one of my strong points."

Impossible Encounters

"In the only way possible. Using the fifth force."

It's not easy to carry on a conversation like this. One must keep a straight face, and there is great temptation to poke fun. It's even harder to suppress the laughter that is ready to bubble to the surface. But through long experience I have become very skilled in self-control.

"The fifth force?" I repeated, expressing the mild surprise I felt appropriate.

"That's what we call it. You know about it, too, but haven't yet recognized it as a force, so you use another name. Actually, it has several names. One of them, for example, is imagination."

This time I didn't have to feign surprise. "Imagination?"

"Yes. Imagination, fantasy, daydreams, whatever you like. The ability to conceive of something that does not seem to exist." He indicated the shelves around us with a broad, sweeping gesture. "All these are the fruit of imagination, aren't they?"

I could only confirm that they were.

"And you are convinced that they are pure fantasy. You feel that there's no way the worlds of science fiction could ever be real. Isn't that right?"

"Well . . . yes. . . ." I mumbled, finding myself in a spot. "I mean, for the most part. . . . Although sometimes, of course, there might be certain coincidences. . . . It's not out of the question. . . . But very rarely. . . ."

"Tell me," he said, putting a stop to my stammering, "how does a work of science fiction originate?"

I didn't reply at once. The conversation had taken a completely unexpected turn. Who would have thought that we'd wind up discussing the problem of literary creation? I have discussed many unusual subjects with the eccentrics who visit me, but never this.

"Well, I don't know exactly. My experience in this regard is quite limited. I have only written a few stories.

I suppose the writer cogitates, and then an idea flashes in his mind and . . ."

"An idea flashes, yes! Do you know what actually happens at that moment—when, as you say, an 'idea flashes', seemingly out of nowhere?"

Of course I didn't know, so I shrugged my shoulders.

"The fifth force is activated!"

The pause that followed was deliberate, a dramatic effect calculated to ensure that the revelation would make the strongest possible impression on me. To demonstrate enlightenment, I nodded sagely.

"Unlike the four fundamental forces that exist on the level of the very simple, the fifth force appears solely on the level of the very complex. It can take effect throughout the cosmos, but in only a single class of locale: in centers of awareness of sufficiently developed species. In your species this center is obviously the brain." The visitor tapped his head with his middle finger.

"Obviously," I readily agreed, tapping my head in fellowship.

"The fifth force is unrestricted by space or time: it acts instantly, by completely cancelling the distance between you, the emitter, and whatever point elsewhere in the cosmos towards which you have directed it. For instance, by activating the fifth force, you are able to see another world as clearly as if you were actually in it."

"I see." The most important thing in such conversations is to give the impression that you accept what you are being told easily and without skepticism. The more outlandish the matter, the more easily you should appear to go along with it.

"That is the idea that flashes. If you don't really know what's going on, that the fifth force has been activated, it will seem that you have made it all up, that nothing is real. But actually, nothing has been invented. The world that suddenly appears in your consciousness is no less real than your own, regardless of how unusual it may appear."

"Very interesting," I commented.

"All these books here are considered fanciful prose, while in my world they would be regarded as commonplace documents of unimpeachable authenticity. Your misconception will be rectified once you have mastered the fifth force, instead of using it in the wild, uncontrolled manner you have until now."

"If I've understood properly, then this would no longer be a bookshop but some sort of . . . archive?"

"Yes, a place where data about other worlds are collected, stored and made available. That is my field of work. I use the fifth force to investigate other worlds and catalogue them. That is how I came across the Earth."

"And so you decided to visit us?"

He shook his head abruptly. "No, no, you don't understand. It wasn't that simple. The fifth force does not transport matter to distant places. Only information. Whoever uses it does not move from his own world."

"But you've come here to Earth, right?"

"That happened because of the interference."

"Interference?"

"Yes. When two fifth force beams overlap."

"Aha, so that's it."

The visitor did not continue right away. He took out his handkerchief again and wiped his face. Several streaks of sweat were now streaming down his forehead, winding their way downwards to lose themselves in his beard. The vegetable smell emanating from him had become more powerful in the course of our conversation, almost intoxicating.

"When I directed my beam towards Earth, something highly unexpected happened. Another beam was heading outwards from here in the opposite direction at the same time. Someone had just flashed an idea about my world. A writer of science fiction, obviously, using the fifth force quite unskillfully, because if he knew the slightest thing about it he would never have let it happen. He would have known how dangerous it is when two beams interfere with each other."

"Dangerous?" I replied, properly aghast.

"Quite so. Two beams that interfere create a gap in the space-time continuum. If this gap is not quickly closed, it will start to suck in everything around it. First of all its two end points, Earth and my world in this case, then the planetary systems to which they belong, and then neighboring star systems. There is actually no end to its voracity. It's as though a black hole has opened up, eleven and a half light years long!"

I could only express appropriate horror. "Why, that's terrible! Horrible! Is there anything that can save us, or are we doomed to annihilation?"

"Yes, there is, if I am able to cancel the interference. It's still not too late for that. But time is running out."

"Then you must not hesitate," I said in haste. "How do you cancel the interference? What needs to be done?"

"I have to find the work about my world. Then go back with it and join it to my documentation about Earth. When these two fifth-force products are joined together, the interference will disappear and the gap will close."

"But how will you go back? Please don't reproach me, but I still don't understand how you got here." This was not exactly in the spirit of my strategy. I usually avoid unnecessary questions, if for no other reason than because they are quite likely to be answered, which needlessly prolongs the conversation. But I felt I owed it to this eccentric somehow. He had taken pains to invent an admirable story, not some tedious inanity like most of the others. Many science fiction writers would envy him for this.

"Through the gap, of course. It can be used as a shortcut until it slips out of control. The crossing is instantaneous. I traversed all those light years in just one move, ending up in front of your bookshop. It was like stepping through to the other side of a kind of mirror, which was a new and very unusual experience even for me. I never thought I would ever go through a fifth-force interference zone. It may not look that way to you, but I am really no adventurer. Although I spend most of my time investigating other worlds, this is the first time I have physically left my own. Actually, I think I am more of what you would call a bookworm."

A rather uncomfortable smile appeared on the man's lips, as though in apology. I returned his smile, feeling suddenly sympathetic towards him. In other circumstances, this could have been an interesting exchange of ideas between two fellow writers, even somewhat kindred souls. I really liked his story. Even the bit about the shortcut wasn't bad. Not exactly original, but convincing nonetheless. As far as I could see, there was only one weak spot in the whole thing. I could have ignored it, but the hairsplitting critic in me prevailed in the end.

"I had no idea," I said, "that there were humans on other worlds, too. Yet so you must be—at least, to judge by your appearance."

"Of course there aren't."

"Well, then, how . . . ?" I asked, indicating his body with my hand.

"Transformation," he replied succinctly, as though this explained everything.

"Ah, of course. I should have thought of it. Under the influence of the fifth force, indubitably."

"That's right. It makes it possible, while it is in interference, if you know how to manage it properly. But only for a short period. That is another reason why I am in a hurry. I won't be able to stay in this shape much

The Bookshop

longer. And I don't feel very happy in it. It's very uncomfortable and clumsy. I don't envy you this body one bit. It's extremely unsuited for movement, in particular."

"Surely there must have been some reason why you couldn't appear here in your own body?"

"Of course. I would die within moments. This is an extremely poisonous atmosphere for me, and the pressure is very high. Rarely have I come across such a dangerous environment, and I am acquainted with a very large number of worlds. But even if the conditions on Earth were perfect, I would still have to take human form. Because of you."

"Because of me?"

A smile played on the visitor's lips again. "Yes, because of you. How do you think you would have reacted if I had appeared in your bookshop in my natural form? Would you be conversing so casually with a ball?"

"A ball?" I repeated. A bell rang softly somewhere in the back of my mind.

"Yes, a ball, perfectly round and soft. What shape is more suitable than a ball in a world completely devoid of uneven spots and obstacles, and covered with dense vegetation? It's almost as if the entire planet were enveloped in a gigantic plant carpet. There is nothing lovelier than rolling on it."

I tried to swallow the lump in my throat, but my throat had suddenly tightened. I could feel my pulse start to pound dully in my ears.

"And what a captivating smell it has! That's what is actually the worst thing about Earth. I could somehow become accustomed to all the rest, but never this foul odor." He sniffed the heated air of the bookshop with disgust. "If you ever had the chance to smell the fragrances of my world, you would never be able to stand it here again."

Impossible Encounters

I feverishly started to think. This wasn't really happening. It could not be happening! There must be some simple explanation. But none that crossed my mind made any sense.

"Smells," the visitor continued inexorably, "that emanate from the diversity of grasses that do not exist on any other of the multitude of worlds I have encountered to date. Lomus, rochum, mirrana, hoon, ameya, oolg, vorona . . ."

". . . pigeya, gorola, olam," I continued with a voice deadened almost to a whisper.

The visitor's face lit up. "So that means you recognize the work!" he cried.

I recognized it, of course. It was truly a new story. So new that it had not yet been published, and thus could not possibly be found on the shelf over there with the recently published works. It was a story that no one but its author should or could know about at this moment. A story that resided, saved several times too many, in the virtual space of my computer.

I nodded briefly, wordlessly.

"Please give it to me. Quickly! If I don't hurry it might be too late."

As I slipped a diskette into the computer with automatic movements and pressed the keys to copy it, questions teemed furiously in my head. But I knew I would not ask any of them. Not only because there was no time left for him to reply, but also because I was not really prepared for the answers.

The visitor took the diskette that I handed him, examined it carefully as though his eyes could see into its contents, then glanced at me and smiled again. He didn't say a word. I tried to smile, too, but it looked more like a grimace.

He turned around and headed hurriedly for the door. A moment later he was swallowed up by the thick wall of fog.

I stood there for a long time, motionless, staring at the impenetrable greyness that had engulfed him. And then my fingers hit the keyboard again. The tangle of letters disappeared from the screen in an instant, leaving behind a yellow void. The story that I had almost finished faded into nothingness. It left no trace behind it, just as the visitor had left no trace behind him. I could pretend to myself that I had never even written it, and that, as on so many other evenings, no one had entered the bookshop once the wispy spirits had made their sluggish ascent from the riverbed.

But I was deprived of this privilege to delude myself. The story had, in fact, been removed—just one erasure had destroyed all earlier saves—but the visitor had left a trace behind him after all. It was very faint, yet undeniable. I noticed it the first time I breathed in deeply through my nose. A tangle of delicate vegetable smells of unknown origin hovered faintly all around me. It might be impalpable to other people, but as long as I could smell it I knew I must restrain myself from writing science fiction.

4. The Train

Mr Pohotny, senior vice president of a bank prominent in the capital city, met God on a train. In a First Class compartment, of course. Mr. Pohotny did not take the train very often, but whenever he did he travelled First Class; it not only reflected and reinforced his social position, it also minimized the probability that he would find himself in unsuitable company. Having a mistrustful and suspicious nature, to which his profession was attuned, he took pains to avoid the company of strangers whenever possible. Indeed, before setting forth this time he had even—guided by some premonition, perhaps—briefly considered reserving all of the compartment's six seats, to ensure that no one would bother him; but his banker's common sense had triumphed over that notion. It would represent too heavy an outlay to obtain something that, with a little luck, he might get quite free.

Luck was with Mr. Pohotny for almost three quarters of the trip. Then, at a small station where fast trains did not normally stop, God climbed into the First Class car and headed straight for Mr. Pohotny's compartment. The senior vice president did not immediately recognize God, of course. Although he couldn't explain exactly why, he thought at first that the gentleman who opened the door to his compartment was a retired army officer, most likely a colonel. He was a short man with greying, though still abundant hair; a trim mustache; slightly florid cheeks. He was wearing

Impossible Encounters

a suit of classic cut that cleverly disguised his somewhat excessive girth.

God entered, and favored Mr. Pohotny with a cordial smile and a brief nod. He took his train ticket out of his left jacket pocket, examined it, sat in the seat next to the window across from Mr. Pohotny, and crossed his legs. Then he looked his fellow traveller over without a word, smiling all the while.

In other circumstances his bearing and demeanor would have greatly annoyed Mr. Pohotny. He would have regarded the man as impolite, even impudent, for it is most unseemly to stare at a complete stranger, and even more to smile broadly while so doing. When he had toyed with the idea of buying up the whole compartment, it was just this sort of unpleasantness he had had in mind. Antisocial behavior was all too common, even in First Class.

Yet for some reason this stranger's staring failed to irritate him—quite the reverse, one might say. He took it as a completely acceptable invitation to talk, thereby shortening the dreary trip. What harm could derive from two polished gentlemen of similar age striking up a conversation, given that Fate had thrown them briefly together? Were they to remain silent until they reached their destination, simply because they had not been formally introduced? Certainly not! One should not be a slave to rigid social conventions.

Mr Pohotny deliberately laid down the book he had been reading on the seat next to him—a leather-bound edition of *Impossible Encounters*—and returned his fellow traveller's smile. "I hope you don't mind the open window," he said.

"Not at all," God replied, "it's very sultry."

"It's often quite sultry during the summer," the senior vice president remarked. Having delivered this truism, he realized that it was hardly a gem of perspicacity. He felt awkward; he was inexperienced in small

The Train

talk. "If you wish, we can raise it a little," he added obligingly.

"No, no," God said, "there's no need, it's quite all right as it is."

"It's better to travel in other seasons," Mr. Pohotny continued after a moment's reflection. "Then it's never sultry, and you don't have to open the window."

"Yes," God agreed, "if you are able to choose, it's better to avoid traveling in the heat."

"Although sometimes in winter they overheat the cars, and then the window has to be opened for a short time, to cool the compartment a bit."

"It's really much nicer when it isn't too hot."

"The worst time, actually, is during the spring and fall. Then it's hardest for the passengers to reach an agreement. Someone always wants to keep the window open a bit for the sake of fresh air, particularly during long trips, while others are bothered by the draft."

God sighed. "It's not easy to satisfy people."

There was nothing to add to or subtract from that conclusion, but it nonetheless put the senior vice president in a predicament. He wanted to continue the conversation, but they seemed to have exhausted the topic of opening the window. Nor did a single further conversational gambit spring to mind. Truly, what are the interests of retired colonels? He had never spent any time in their company, so he had no insight into their tastes. They must be interested in military matters. What else? Unfortunately, Mr. Pohotny lacked the slightest understanding of the arts of war.

God continued to stare at him, with his fixed little smile. The senior vice president had already started to fidget, when he suddenly saw a way out of this predicament. Of course! Now was the right time to make each other's acquaintance. That would certainly help to unburden their mutual reserve.

He bowed, perhaps somewhat more deeply than was

customary. "Let me introduce myself," he said, extending his hand towards the figure opposite. "Pohotny, banker, senior vice president."

God shook the extended hand, bowed in response, and replied succinctly, without the blemish of superfluous additions: "God."

If anything surprised the senior vice president, even briefly, it was the fact that he wasn't the least surprised to learn the identity of his travelling companion. All at once it seemed not only obvious but even quite natural that the heavy-set, grey-haired gentleman in the dark suit across from him should be God. Of course, who else? Where had he got the nonsensical idea that he was some sort of retired colonel? Quite inappropriate!

Despite the surprising composure with which he received this information, Mr. Pohotny remained somewhat embarrassed. He had even less to say to God than to a retired colonel. It was immediately clear, however, that small talk would be quite out of place; besides, he had already displayed his lack of skill at it. He also felt that banking was not the proper subject, either, however expert his approach. No, he had to find something more suitable.

"Am I dead?" he asked, a little taken aback, finally letting go of God's hand.

"Dead? No, why do you think you're dead?"

"Well, I thought people only met you after death. At least, that's what they say."

"They say all kinds of things. You shouldn't believe everything you hear. To begin with, I meet everyone once while they're alive."

"I didn't know that."

"Of course you didn't. No one knows anything about it."

The senior vice president nodded slowly. Then he took a handkerchief out of his pocket and wiped his forehead, keeping the handkerchief in his hand once he

The Train

had finished. "There must be a reason for these meetings, I suppose?"

"Yes, there is."

"Does it have to do with what people do, how they behave? Whether they're honest or not?"

"No," God replied. "Such considerations have no bearing upon it."

Mr Pohotny tried to hide his sigh of relief, but was only partially successful. "Then might I know your reasons for meeting people?"

"Of course. To answer their questions."

"What questions?"

"Any they may have. They can ask anything."

"Anything?"

"Yes. You can ask me whatever you want. Absolutely no holds barred."

The senior vice president thought for a moment. "And what is expected in return?"

"Nothing."

"Nothing at all?"

"Nothing at all. I'm not the devil. Take this as, let's say, rectifying an injustice. As God, I am supposed to be just, am I not? People are deprived of many things, so this is my chance to make up for it a little. At absolutely no cost to you."

"So, that's it," Mr. Pohotny said. "Very generous of you. I admit, I haven't been excessively devout, so to speak, but in the future, rest assured, I . . ."

"Don't act rashly. Wait and see whether you like what you hear. It's not always the case, and piety has a tendency to evaporate. So, what would you like to ask me?"

The senior vice president stopped twisting the damp handkerchief in his hand. "This is all so sudden. If only I had time to think it over a little, to prepare for it! It's not easy to be called upon to ask God something like this, out of a clear blue sky."

Impossible Encounters

"Surely, there must be something you would like to find out, something that intrigues you, even obsesses you? Don't hesitate for a moment! I will answer any question you ask."

"It's hard to decide. There are things that clearly interest me, but . . ."

"I must draw your attention to the fact that we don't have much time. Your station isn't very far away, and I will get off the train before you. I advise you to use this meeting to your very best advantage. There won't be another."

"Well, all right, here goes. As you see, I am on my way to evaluate the reliability of a company that has asked our bank for a loan. A huge loan, almost one-third of our capital. I carry a great responsibility. If I recommend approval of the loan and it falls through, it would be a serious blow for the bank, perhaps disastrous. In any case, it would be the end of my career. On the other hand, if I turn down the loan and the job succeeds with the help of some other bank, I will completely lose my reputation. It would therefore be of invaluable assistance to know how to act."

The smile disappeared from God's face. "Are you sure you want to ask that?"

"Yes," the senior vice president replied without hesitation. "It is a very serious matter. I have never had to make such an important decision before. My whole career is at stake, and quite possibly the future of the bank too."

"All right. As you wish. You might have asked me a more general, ultimate, even transcendent question, but if you're not interested in that . . ."

"Of course I am!" Mr. Pohotny objected, interrupting God. "I think about such things occasionally, indeed I do, but, you see, at this moment . . ."

"I see, I see," God broke him off, "you don't have to explain anything. Here is the answer to your question.

Your evaluation will be that you should approve the loan, and you will not be mistaken."

This time the senior vice president did not attempt to suppress his sigh of relief. He was even briefly tempted to cross himself, but it seemed somehow improper. "Thank you so much. I shall certainly become very devout, you can count on that."

"Perhaps, but not for long. Just a year and a half."

"What do you mean? Nothing will be able to divert me from my faith! I assure you that I shall remain devout to the end of my life."

"That's what I'm talking about. You have a year and a half of life."

Mr Pohotny squinted at his travelling companion. "But that's not possible," he said finally in a hushed voice. "I mean, I'm completely healthy, I go to the doctor regularly for a checkup, I lead an orderly life. . . ."

"People die of other things than illness. You, for instance, will commit suicide. You will shoot yourself. A single, large-caliber bullet into your right temple."

The senior vice president raised his handkerchief to his mouth and wiped the corners with trembling movements. "Why would I do that?"

"Because you will make a mistake that will lead to your bank's ruin. In the wake of your forthcoming triumph you will become over-confident, and in circumstances similar to these you will make the wrong decision. Suicide will be your only honorable way out."

Not knowing how to respond to this, Mr. Pohotny continued to stare dully at the figure on the seat across from him, his pulse beating in his ears. But then a thought flashed through his febrile mind, and he grabbed at it.

"But that can be avoided! You have warned me of the danger. What if I don't make any decision? What if I withdraw completely from the bank?"

"You won't be able to rely on my warning, I'm afraid," God replied. "Remember I told you that no one knows of my meetings with humans during their lives. Why do you think that is?"

The senior vice president shrugged. "Because it's a secret?"

"No. That wouldn't work. Someone would have discovered it by now. That's human nature. I had to provide something more reliable. No one remembers meeting me. You will also forget it completely as soon as I leave the train."

"Then, if you don't mind, what is the purpose of meeting with people? You offer them answers that they cannot remember?"

"That was the most that could be done. The choice was between leaving human beings in permanent ignorance, and giving them knowledge that is paid for by being immediately erased. Between nothing and something, I chose something. It seemed to be more just."

"It doesn't seem very just to me, to tell a man that he will soon die, and then deprive him of the chance to save himself! Don't be cross with me, but that is more what I would expect of the devil."

"On the contrary. The devil would happily deprive you of oblivion, because that would afford him the opportunity to revel in your agony. But even if you remembered this meeting, you would still not be able to extricate yourself. Nothing you could do would prevent the ineluctable unfolding of ordained events. Why, then, expose you to the unnecessary anguish that must derive from knowledge of your approaching death?"

From a distance came the protracted whistle of the locomotive, as the train began to slow down.

"I might have asked something else," Mr. Pohotny reflected softly.

"Yes, you might have. But now it's too late, unfortunately. This is my station coming up."

"It's not easy to find the right question to ask God."

"I know. But if it's any consolation, it is also hard to satisfy people, as we had already concluded." God stood up and offered his hand to the senior vice president. "Goodbye, Mr. Pohotny. It was a pleasure to meet you."

Mr Pohotny stood up and shook the proffered hand. "Goodbye," he replied, although it seemed to him that the word was not quite suited to the moment.

When the train started moving several minutes later, the senior vice president raised his eyes from the book which he continued to read and briefly looked out of the window, wondering why they had made an unscheduled stop at this small station. But it made no difference, since there would be no more stops until his destination. Now it was certain that he would be alone in the compartment to the end of his trip. Wisely had he decided not to buy up all the seats! A successful bank vice president must make the proper decision at all times. This was a good omen for the evaluation he must shortly make.

5. The Confessional

THE DEEP, HARSH COUGHING that came from the other compartment of the confessional sounded almost like a distant growl.

The priest started in confusion and raised his eyes towards the gap in the partition that separated his cubicle from the area where the faithful kneel to confess. Through the slanted wickerwork that served as a semitransparent screen, he detected the outlines of a heavy-set man. He hadn't heard him enter because he had been asleep. He had secreted himself in the confessional for that specific purpose, not because he was waiting for a penitent. Here, this failing of his was least noticeable. It would not do to have a visitor catch him asleep in the open part of the church.

His conscience did not bother him overly on account of this sin. He found partial justification in his advanced age, which enhanced the periodic temptation to sleep during the day, particularly in the middle of the afternoon when the church was very quiet. But the faithful were equally to blame. If there were more of them, if they had not thinned out so much, he would not have had time for this improper repose. When he'd come to this parish many years ago as a young priest, the situation had been completely different. At that time he would never have been left alone in the church for so long. But now a secular age held ruthless sway. Recently, there had even been days when not a single person crossed the church's threshold.

Impossible Encounters

There was one more extenuating circumstance that mitigated the sin of sleeping in the confessional. Whenever he felt his eyelids close, he would not simply go through the thick, dark-red velvet curtain as if into a sleeping berth; rather he would go with the worthy intention of reading—although once he drew the curtain it was rather dark inside, at least for his eyesight which was already quite poor.

In the beginning he had taken the Bible with him as the most appropriate reading material for such a context. But since he never got beyond half a page before sleep engulfed him, that seemed some sort of sacrilege, so he came to substitute other, less holy works for the sacred text. That, to be sure, did not seem to be the solution most respectful to God and His house either, but since this reading was of equally brief duration, the offence was not very great. In any case, he had never been unduly strict in granting absolution to others, so why be harsh with himself?

Startled out of sleep, he forgot for a moment that there was an open book in his lap. When he twitched, it slipped and fell to the floor, landing with a dull thud. He quickly bent down, picked it up and tucked it under his mantle. There was no way the visitor in the other compartment could have seen it, of course, yet he suddenly felt like a boy who has been caught looking at indecent pictures. The book that had for quite some time been his companion whenever he withdrew to the confessional for his afternoon nap was not indecent in the slightest; at least, not to judge by the few early pages that he had managed to read. Even so, its title—*Impossible Encounters*—seemed rather inappropriate for the Lord's house.

"I hear you, my son," he said, after clearing his throat. He wondered if he knew the man. Only a few still confessed more or less regularly, and he could easily recognize each of them by voice.

The Confessional

"Did I come at an inconvenient time?" It was the deep, velvety voice of a man somewhere in his middle years. He had never heard it before.

"No time is inconvenient to visit the church. God's ear is constantly receptive to those who would speak to Him. When was the last time you confessed, my son?"

The answer from the other side of the window was not immediate, as though the visitor was intently searching through his memory. "A very long time ago," he said at last.

"That is not good," replied the priest with mild reproach in his voice. "The soul must not endure the weight of accumulated sins for very long. Confession brings release and forgiveness."

"There can be no forgiveness for my sins," said the visitor in an even, casual voice, as though stating a truism.

"Certainly there is. God has infinite mercy. There is no sin that will not be forgiven if one is sincerely penitent."

"Yes, there is. My sins will certainly never be forgiven. But it makes no difference. I'm not at all sorry for them."

"Do not speak like that, my son. Everyone cares whether their sins will be forgiven. Do you want your soul to end up in Hell?"

"Why not? It's not as bad as people think."

The priest turned his eyes towards the bulky figure in the neighboring compartment, even though he could still see nothing distinct through the dense wickerwork.

"It's not bad in Hell?" he repeated slowly, emphasizing each word. "It's terrible even to think something like that, let alone say it. Are you at all aware of what you have just said, my son?"

"Perfectly aware. I know from my own experience. I just came from there."

"Where did you come from?" the priest asked softly, after a short pause.

Impossible Encounters

"From Hell."

The priest shook his head. Here was yet another deplorable offspring of the secular age. He had already met others like him in this place. It was not enough for them to be non-believers; they came to the church specifically to blaspheme. But he knew how to handle them. It was for just such lost souls that he should fight the hardest. That the man had come here at all showed that all was not completely hopeless.

"No man has ever returned from Hell," he said didactically, like a teacher pointing out a simple, obvious truth to a backward child. "The Tempter would never allow it."

"He wouldn't, I agree. But that doesn't apply to me."

"Oh? Why not, if you please?"

"Because I am not a man."

The shroud of afternoon silence suddenly settled on the confessional. So this is what it's all about, the priest thought gloomily. Before him was not just an ordinary, contumacious non-believer, but one of those poor wretches whose clumsy wrestling with matters of faith had upset their minds. He hadn't met one of that kind in a long time, and they usually identified with the Savior. As far as he could remember, this *soi-disant* Devil was a personal first for him. So he had to proceed carefully, without ill-mannered contradictions, yet with firmness. In the end he might succeed in bringing the man to his senses, though it was certainly not going to be easy.

"So, that's it," he replied with studied calm, as if this were an everyday encounter. "You are the Tempter himself, if I understand correctly. He is the only one who is allowed to leave Hell."

The head on the other side of the wickerwork gave a brief nod. "You understand correctly."

The priest brushed the tips of his fingers across his wrinkled brow and sighed. "Very nice, but there is

The Confessional

one problem. The Tempter would never dare cross the threshold of God's house."

"You think not? That is only one of the many prejudices against me. It is here that I have always felt most comfortable."

"Strange. How is it, then, that no one has ever seen you? It would be hard for your manifestation to pass unnoticed."

"Manifestation? Oh, the tail, horns, hooves, goat's head and all the rest? That is all pure nonsense, of course. No one notices me because I look quite ordinary, unassuming. Like you, for example."

The priest squinted to sharpen his vision a little, but the figure on the other side of the window still presented only a vague, incomplete outline.

"If you look quite ordinary, how can you convince people that you are who you make yourself out to be? Couldn't just anyone appear and claim to be the Tempter?"

"They could, yes. That even happens from time to time. But it doesn't work for long. Sooner or later they have to offer proof to support their claim."

"And you can offer that proof?"

"Of course."

"That might be, for example, an infernal fire that suddenly breaks out in the middle of the church, with all manner of freaks and monsters streaming out of it? Or maybe the stone floor would split asunder, revealing a chasm that leads straight to your red-hot throne?"

The visitor did not reply at once, and the priest thought he might have gone too far. If he wanted to help the poor man, he shouldn't appear to be making fun of him.

"It would not be anything so unrefined, so primitive, of course," the deep voice retorted from the neighboring compartment. "There is no need for that. Such ideas about me serve only to arouse needless fears in

Impossible Encounters

the ignorant. There is much more subtle and convincing proof."

"Would you perhaps show me some?"

"With pleasure."

From somewhere on the opposite side of the church, near the entrance, came the soft tapping of footsteps. The priest's trained ear told him it must be a woman, probably young, heading towards one of the last rows of benches. She sat down and immediately started to pray.

When everything fell silent once again, the visitor continued, "Let me ask you the same question you asked me at the beginning. When was the last time you confessed?"

"Me? I confess every day. If I didn't, how could I have the right to hear the confessions of others?"

"You confess to yourself, I assume, since you are the only priest in this parish?"

"That's right. My conscience is my best confessor. I can't hide anything from it."

"Your conscience, yes. But there are two pitfalls with regard to your conscience. First of all, it can be very lenient, very indulgent. It doesn't bother you too much that, for example, you sleep in the confessional."

I must have been snoring, the priest thought. There's no other way he could have found that out. He came in and heard me snoring. I'll have to do something about that.

"Falling asleep in the confessional once is only an ordinary human weakness, and no heinous sin. I feel remorse, of course."

"Just once?"

The priest grimaced. Somehow, he had lost control of the conversation. Usually he was the one to ask such questions here.

"All right, it might have happened a few other times. But I do not claim to be a perfect saint."

The Confessional

"Although you might be able to make that claim, considering the second problem with your conscience."

"Second problem?"

"Yes. Your conscience can be rather forgetful. If something doesn't please it very much, if it has a hard time finding justification for something, it has a tendency to discard it, to pretend it never happened. A real confessor should never act like that, wouldn't you agree?"

"I'm afraid I don't quite understand," the priest admitted after a short hesitation.

"It might be clearer to you if I explain it by means of an example. What would your conscience do if you were oppressed by feelings of guilt for the loss of two lives? Would it constantly remind you of that, make your life unbearable, or would it prefer to push the whole thing under the rug?"

The priest felt something tighten in his throat. Who was this man? Why had he come here? What did he want from him?

"I don't know. I can't even imagine that. I am not haunted by feelings of guilt for the loss of two lives."

"That is obvious. Although you should be. A conscience that is inclined to forget can still grant you forgiveness, but that doesn't count for very much, I'm afraid. There is another, much more important forgiveness, and nothing is forgotten there. It remembers everything and takes everything into consideration. Every tiny little thing."

"What are you talking about, my son?"

"I think you know perfectly well what I'm talking about. Your conscience does not really forget, it merely represses things. But that works only until someone reminds you of what you have repressed. As I am doing right now."

"Reminding me of what?" Though the priest tried to keep his voice firm, it began to quiver.

Impossible Encounters

"Of the girl who drowned after jumping off the bridge. Five months pregnant. After finding out that the father of her child, a young priest she had fallen in love with, would not keep his promise. That he would not renounce his vows for her."

The sound of footfalls came once again from the entrance to the church. The young woman had finished her short prayer and was now leaving. She walked with quick steps, hurrying somewhere.

The priest could find no words for a while, staring fixedly at the thick, dark pleats of the curtain in front of him. At first he wanted to protest, to deny this terrible accusation, to challenge the identity of the large figure in the neighboring compartment. But he did not. There would be no sense in that. The memory, suddenly freed from the deepest, darkest corner of his mind, washed over him as violently as the icy water into which the girl had plunged so long ago. Not only had he turned his back on her, he had been unable to attend the funeral. The church does not give shelter to suicides. They are not even given a place in the cemetery. He never found out where she was buried.

No one ever suspected that he was to blame for the girl's demise. They had taken great pains to keep their relationship secret, and she had left no letter of farewell in which she might have accused him, thus making his infidelity all the worse. He remained blameless in the world of men, but certainly not before his own self. After great torment, he had finally repressed the memory, yet he knew quite well it was only temporary, that a true settlement of accounts awaited. Now the time had come. The Tempter had come to claim his due. The priest had no right to expect mercy for what he had done. He did not actually even want mercy. There was only one place for his soul.

"So Hell isn't as bad as people think?" he said at last, in a barely audible voice.

The Confessional

"It isn't. But you won't have the chance to find out for yourself."

"What do you mean?" He was just about to add the usual "my son", but stopped himself at the last moment.

"Your soul will go to Heaven."

The priest raised bewildered eyes towards the window, even though by now he knew he would never see his interlocutor any better.

"How could such a terribly sinful soul as mine go to Heaven? That certainly cannot and must not happen!"

"But it will nonetheless. I will make sure of it."

"Why? I don't understand. . . ."

"What benefit would I get from your soul? Almost none. Hell is already packed with sinners like you. You might even say we're overcrowded. Whenever I take a new lost soul, I'm only doing God a favor. I relieve Him of what He doesn't like. I take a bad creation out of His sight, so He can maintain the illusion that everything He's done is flawless. Why should I do that? Why should I play into His hands? We are opponents, not allies, right? I should do everything I can to injure Him, to remind Him constantly that the world He has created is imperfect. And what better reminder than to surround Him with the worst of sinners?"

"But He will never allow that."

"He will. He will have no choice."

"God will have no choice?"

"Yes. He's not quite as almighty as people think. For example, He could never exile from Heaven a soul that knows nothing of its sins, regardless of how great they are. Sending such a pure soul to Hell would be infinitely unjust. And God is proud of His justice, right?"

"I am perfectly aware of my sin."

"Yes, but not for much longer. That is why I came here."

"Why?"

"To remove your memory of the sin you committed."

"I don't want to forget it."

"What was the repression you resorted to until now? Another form of oblivion, correct? But incomplete. Now I will give you perfect, complete oblivion. You will no longer remember anything that might burden you. Everything will be permanently erased. No one will be able to convince you that you have committed any sin whatsoever. When you stand before God, your soul will be the incarnation of purity. You haven't actually the slightest reason to complain. The gates of Heaven will be open to you. What else did you dare hope for that could be any sweeter? Although, to tell you the truth, I don't envy you much."

The priest quickly rose from his seat in the narrow compartment. He suddenly felt enclosed in an upright coffin.

"You must not do that! I must go to Hell! That would be terribly unjust. . . ."

"Probably. But I am sure you understand that such considerations carry no weight with me."

The priest reached for the curtain. He did not know what he wanted to do. It was an instinctive move, a feverish attempt to find refuge, to escape somehow from the trap into which he had fallen. But his hand never touched the velvet. It sagged next to his body, which collapsed back onto the chair. The drowsiness that suddenly engulfed him was not his usual afternoon slump, rather something very deep, something he had never felt before. It had to take over at once, he didn't even have the strength to open his book, let alone read a few lines. His eyes closed by themselves and his head drooped on his chest.

If he had any dreams, he could not remember them when he woke up. He remained sitting there a few moments, gathering his wits, and then pushed aside the curtain and left the confessional. There was no one

The Confessional

in the church. He always felt refreshed after this short rest, but what now filled him was not just renewed vigor. The thought crossed his mind that this was the spiritual state in which it would be most suitable to stand before God: tranquil, at peace with the world, with an unblemished conscience. Like the righteous. He turned slowly toward the aisle between the rows of benches to greet the light pouring from the entrance.

6. The Atelier

When the front doorbell rang, the silence in my atelier seemed to implode, like a balloon that has suddenly lost all its air.

I turned away from the computer screen where I had been sitting for a long time, and looked at the door in bewilderment. Before I start to write, I always turn off both the telephone and the intercom. It is impossible to reach me then. If someone calls me on the phone, they will think I'm away from home, or don't want to answer, and if someone rings at the entrance to the building downstairs, I won't hear it at all and will thus be unable to let them in. But someone had obviously entered, someone whom I hadn't let in, and who was now standing in front of my door.

I got up irritably and headed for the front door of the atelier. I can't stand being interrupted while working. No one has the right to disturb me, particularly now that my time is running out. I couldn't imagine who it might be. It certainly could not be someone from the building dropping by for a visit, because I had not cultivated even the most attenuated friendship with any of my neighbors. The most I do is to exchange polite remarks on the rare occasions I meet someone in the hall or elevator. I don't even know the names of the people who live on my floor.

Maybe it was a door-to-door salesman who had somehow entered the building and was now peddling from apartment to apartment, offering something I

Impossible Encounters

certainly didn't need. I should have stayed at my desk, without giving myself away. Even the most persistent intruder would give up after a while, concluding that there was no one home. But since I had already gone to the door, I put my eye to the peephole and peered out. I realized just then that I had never done this before, simply because there had been no need to check out any visitor. I always knew who was ringing the bell.

In front of the door to my atelier stood a distinctly elderly gentleman. He was short and thin, wearing a hat and a dark coat, and a dark-red bow tie. I had never seen him before. He couldn't have been a door-to-door salesman, not only because of his advanced age, but also because he was not carrying any bag for whatever he might have been selling. All he was holding was a rather small book. He took off his hat and bowed to me, and I moved back from the peephole in embarrassment. I'd had no idea that you could tell from the outside when someone was looking through it.

There was no longer any sense in pretending I wasn't there. I had to open the door; but whatever happened, I was determined it should be brief. The gentleman had undoubtedly made a mistake. He had surely come to visit someone else in the building, and then turned up at my door by mistake, for it had no nameplate on it. I could not, however, be of much assistance in directing him to wherever he wanted to go.

"Hello," I said, opening the door halfway. "May I help you?"

The man did not reply at once. He just looked at me, smiling slightly. We stood like that in silence for a few moments.

"Don't you recognize me?" he said at last. He had a rough, elderly voice, but with an element of good cheer.

"I'm afraid not," I replied in surprise. "Should I?"

"I believe so. Who else, if not you?"

"Please don't hold it against me," I said after a short

The Atelier

hesitation, "but I don't seem to recall when we met. Would you please remind me? With whom do I have the honor?"

Holding his hat in his hand, the old man bowed again. "I cannot tell you my name, unfortunately, since you did not give me one. I am a character from one of your stories who remained nameless. But so it is with many of your characters, is it not?"

I sized up the stranger angrily. "I don't know what you want, sir, or why you came here," I said, raising my voice a little, "but I certainly don't have time for tasteless jokes. You have interrupted me in the middle of very important work. Such conduct is not tolerated in polite society. Please leave."

I started to close the door, but his next words halted me.

"Your work is important, but you're making heavy weather of it."

"Excuse me?" The door that was almost shut opened a crack.

"Your writing. You have written five stories, and would like one more, a final one. Without it your book will be incomplete. But you seem to have run out of inspiration. Not a single letter has appeared on your screen for days, and you can afford to fritter away no more time, isn't that so?"

"Who are you? What is the meaning of this?" I tried to sound sharp, even wrathful, but a quaver in my voice betrayed me.

"I am someone you might find useful. If, of course, you invite me in." He looked briefly from side to side. "It would not be quite proper to talk about it here, in front of the door."

I made no move, not knowing what to do. This whole business was completely insane. The old man standing in front of me clearly could not be who he claimed to be, but, on the other hand, he could not possibly have known what he had just said. No one knew that but

Impossible Encounters

me. The seconds moved ponderously, crushing me with their growing weight.

"Maybe this will dispel your doubts," my visitor said at last, handing me the book he was holding.

I took it hesitantly, thinking as I did that it was irrational. I should cut off this senseless encounter at once, simply close the door without further ado; maybe even slam it shut. You have to act firmly with oddballs, even those of polished demeanor and advanced years. But curiosity, plus a certain vague premonition, prevailed over rationality.

It was a paperback book, not very thick, with a shiny, plastic-laminated cover. I turned the front over and squinted at it. Under my name was the title in large letters: *Impossible Encounters*.

I raised my bewildered eyes to the elderly gentleman, who was still smiling. I realized that I was expected to say something, but nothing coherent crossed my mind. This book could not exist, if only because it had yet to be written. The last chapter was missing. The computer screen on which it was supposed to appear gaped behind me, completely white.

"Where did you get this?" I finally stammered.

"May I not come in?" the stranger persisted.

I hesitated for just a moment before opening the door almost fully and stepping back. The old man passed by me, then stopped in my small hall. At first I didn't understand why he had done this, then I realized what was expected of me.

"With your permission," I said and took his hat, then his long, heavy coat. I had to put the book under my arm briefly in order to hang them on the coat rack next to the front door. "After you," I said, indicating the atelier's main room.

Once inside, the visitor turned this way and that, looking around but saying nothing, just nodding his head. He was wearing a dark blue suit of old-fashioned cut with wide lapels. A handkerchief matching his bow tie peeped delicately from his upper jacket pocket. He waited for me to invite him to sit down, then chose the couch to the right of the door. I was momentarily uncertain as to where I myself should sit, and then I chose the armchair next to the desk, under the lamp with the large yellow shade, so that we faced each other.

"Where did you get this?" I asked, repeating the question that had not been answered.

"From you, of course."

"From me?"

"Yes, you left the book on the coffee table next to the jug and the two glasses. In the room that is entered from the hallway with portraits. Several drops fell on the cover as I was pouring water. Surely you remember?"

I shook my head slowly, more in disbelief than because I could not remember.

He indicated the book in my hand. "In the first story. The first chapter, in fact. 'The Window'."

I opened the book and started to leaf through it with stiff movements. It was truly there, on the seventh page: "1. THE WINDOW". I read the short introductory sentence and then looked at my visitor again.

"As you know," he continued, "I am not exceptional in this regard. The other characters were given the book, too. It appears in each of the stories, although not always the same edition. The Old Man is sitting on it at the top of the ascent, above the clouds. The Bookseller has it on the shelf among his recent acquisitions. The Banker is reading it on the train. And finally, the Priest carries it with him when he withdraws into the confessional for his afternoon nap. You did well to give it to us. If it weren't for the book, this encounter could not have taken place. Regardless which of us came here, you would never have let him inside unless he could present the book."

"But none of that is real. I mean . . ." I knew quite

well what I wanted to say, but for some reason I suddenly couldn't put it into words.

"But what is real? Didn't you write *Impossible Encounters* in order to show that there is no distinct boundary separating the real from the unreal? In any case, were we to stick unconditionally to the real, we would be unable to help you at all."

"Help me?"

"Yes. What did the doctor tell you—how much more time do you have? Two, at most three months, isn't that so?"

"How do you know?" My voice had dropped almost to a whisper.

"We know all about you, of course. That is quite natural. No one knows a writer as well as the characters from his own books. Just as you know us perfectly well, when it comes right down to it."

My head was spinning slowly. One part of my consciousness was still trying to make some sort of sense of all this, but in vain. I had canceled my entitlement to any acceptable sense the moment I got up from my desk and headed for the door to see who was there. And maybe even quite a bit earlier, in fact. Back when I wrote the first sentence of *Impossible Encounters*.

"How would you be able help me?" I asked, my voice still low. "If you know what the doctor told me, then it must be clear to you that there is no reprieve. Soon I will have to go back to the hospital, and this time I will never leave it."

"There is no reprieve, yes, but only in the medical sense. That is not what this is about, however."

"Then what is it about?"

"You will soon die physically, and that is inevitable, alas. But you might join us beforehand."

"Join you?"

"That's right."

"How can I do that?"

The Atelier

"It's quite simple. You want to add one more chapter to *Impossible Encounters*, isn't that so? Fine, write a story about yourself as a writer. Introduce yourself into it as a character."

"What would I gain by that? I mean, it would just be . . . let me put it this way, dead letters on paper. Unreal . . ." It was not until after that last word had trailed away into silence that I realized how gauche it sounded.

The elderly gentleman gave me a reproachful look from the couch. "Do I seem unreal?"

"Well, no, but . . ."

"You see, the fact is you don't really know absolutely everything about us. You undoubtedly think that we have no other existence outside of the limited work in which we appear. But that, of course, is untrue."

"Untrue?"

"Quite. We actually spend relatively little time in the roles of your characters. We are only there when someone reads a story about us. We are best regarded as actors who periodically appear onstage and act the same part in the same play, every time. When no one is reading us, when there is no play, we do not cease to exist, as you have incorrectly assumed." He stopped for a moment, and his smile widened. "We do not turn into dead letters on paper. Quite the contrary. That is when we retire to a large drawing room."

"Where?"

"To a large drawing room. It is very beautiful, as you will see for yourself quite soon. It is cool and quiet. There are lots of comfortable chairs, tables with bowls full of ripe fruit, a piano in the corner, an enormous library. There is also a broad terrace with two well grown potted palms from which a magnificent view stretches towards the sea. To sit there is very pleasant. The sun is always at twilight, so it's not too hot. The only drawback is that we can never go outside. We have to stay

Impossible Encounters

close by because you never know when a new play will start."

"What do you do, penned up inside there? Aren't you bored to death as you wait for the next . . . play?"

"Bored? Not in the least! We know very well how to fill up our free time. It would be much better to call it gracious leisure. Primarily, we carry on interesting, stimulating discussions. We all enjoy them, and I think you will like them, too. In addition, each of us has a talent that serves to entertain the others. My collocutor from 'The Window', for example, plays the piano. He often accompanies those who sing for us. The gentleman who fulfills the demanding role of God in 'The Train' has a truly magnificent voice, while the Tempter from 'The Confessional' is an exquisite painter. I'm sure you will be fascinated by his oils, particularly his still lifes. The older character from 'The Cone' is a most astute thinker, you might even say a philosopher, and we listen to his lectures with rapt attention and curiosity. And there is also a writer, who periodically reads his latest pages to us. Can you guess who that is?"

I shrugged my shoulders after thinking for a moment. "I'm sure I wouldn't know."

"The man who plays the alien in 'The Bookshop'. His style is rather similar to yours, which is not, perhaps, surprising. You will be able to exchange experiences with him. It will be exciting to listen to your discussions." The older gentleman paused again. "But you have deprived us in one sense," he said regretfully.

I looked at him, perplexed. "Which one?"

"There are too few female characters. It would be much nicer for all of us if there were a few more ladies. Couldn't at least one of the main characters have been female?"

"What do you mean—several more ladies? There isn't a single female character in *Impossible Encounters*. Although, of course, that is quite by accident. If I could

The Atelier

have imagined all of this, I certainly would have introduced a woman. My other books are full of female characters."

"There is one woman, though. You forgot the girl who enters the church while the priest and the Tempter are talking in 'The Confessional'."

"But you can't see her. Only her footsteps are heard."

"What difference does that make? In any case, she is the only one who could make those feminine footsteps. You'll understand that when you see her. Let me tell you a secret. We are all in love with her. It is quite certain that you will be no exception."

"Maybe I can still fix things," I said hurriedly, in an apologetic voice. "The last story hasn't been written yet. I could introduce another woman into it."

"But it has already been written. It is here in the book you are holding. The final story, unfortunately, has no women in it."

I stared at my guest several moments, at a loss for words; disturbing questions tumbled through my head. And then I opened the book and started to leaf through it again.

But I did not reach the place I wanted. I was interrupted by the sharp voice of the visitor, who suddenly got up off the couch. "Don't do it! You must not look at the last story until you write it. If you read it in advance, it would be as if the story were writing itself. That would destroy an order of things that nothing should be allowed to endanger. Should that happen, you would never be able to join us. Please give me back my *Impossible Encounters*."

I did not comply at once. It was only with great restraint that I stopped when I was somewhere in the middle of the book. I was spurred by a violent impulse to take at least a peek at the first page of the last story, to see how it started. I was aware that this would have been cheating of some sort, although I might not have been able to explain what kind exactly. This was not, however, why I stopped. Ethical considerations were not enough to overcome the frustration that was devouring me inside, quite as destructively as the disease that would soon curtail my days. The constricting helplessness I felt derived from the knowledge that my time was inexorably running out, while the monitor on my desk remained hopelessly, undeniably empty: death would come faster than inspiration.

What had made me finally stand up and reluctantly hand the book back to the old man was the hope I suddenly felt. It was deeply irrational, earnest and desperate—but all I had left. The faint hope of the writer that what he has written will afford him refuge from the ultimate void.

"I can't do it," I said in a quavering voice. "I've been trying for so long, but nothing comes. Soon the pains will begin. . . ."

A smile returned to the visitor's face. "Of course you can. Believe me. Here is the proof, after all." He raised the little book he had taken from me. "I must go now. You need peace if you are to write. And I can't stay away from the drawing room for long. The plays are about to begin."

We headed towards the front door. I held his coat for him in the hall, then handed him his hat. He placed it on his head with a skilled movement, then extended his hand. Thin, bony as it was, his handshake was firm. And more than that. Friendly. Encouraging. "See you soon," the elderly gentleman said, with a brief bow.

I returned the bow, but said nothing. I closed the door behind my guest and stood there for a while in front of it, staring blankly into space. Then I turned and slowly headed for my desk. The large monitor was waiting with its white emptiness, as though mocking me.

I placed my fingers lightly on the keys, barely touching them. I did not start to type right away. All at once

The Atelier

I was no longer in a hurry. The story now stood before me, formed, final, whole. Almost palpable. All I had to do was write it. I wanted this moment to last as long as possible.

Finally, a dense, buzzing swarm of letters started to fly on the upper part of the screen, appearing, so it seemed, from out of nowhere:

When the front doorbell rang, the silence in my atelier seemed to implode, like a balloon that has suddenly lost all its air. . . .

Contributors

About the author

Zoran Živković was born in Belgrade, Serbia, on October 5, 1948. Until his retirement in 2017, he was a full professor at the Faculty of Philology, the University of Belgrade, teaching creative writing.

He is one of the most translated contemporary Serbian writers: by the end of 2018 there were 106 foreign editions of his books of fiction, published in 23 countries, in 20 languages.

Živković has won several literary awards for his fiction. In 1994 his novel *The Fourth Circle* won the Miloš Crnjanski award. In 2003, Živković's mosaic novel *The Library* won a World Fantasy Award for Best Novella. In 2007 his novel *The Bridge* won the Isidora Sekulić award. In 2007 Živković received the Stefan Mitrov Ljubiša award for his life achievement in literature. In 2014 and 2015 Živković received three awards for his contribution to the literature of fantastika: Art-Anima, Stanislav Lem and The Golden Dragon.

Zoran Živković has been recognized with his selection as European Grand Master for 2017 by the European Science Fiction Society at the 39th Eurocon in Dortmund, Germany.

Živković is the author of 22 books of fiction:
    The Fourth Circle (1993)
    Time Gifts (1997)
    The Writer (1998)
    The Book (1999)
    Impossible Encounters (2000)
    Seven Touches of Music (2001)
    The Library (2002)
    Steps through the Mist (2003)
    Hidden Camera (2003)
    Compartments (2004)
    Four Stories till the End (2004)
    Twelve Collections and the Teashop (2005)
    The Bridge (2006)
    Miss Tamara, The Reader (2006),
    Amarcord (2007)
    The Last Book (2007)
    Escher's Loops (2008)
    The Ghostwriter (2009)
    The Five Wonders of the Danube (2011)
    The Grand Manuscript (2012)
    The Compendium of the Dead (2015)
    The Image Interpreter (2016)

About the artist

Youchan Ito was born 1968 in Aichi prefecture, Japan. She launched her career as a graphic designer in 1988, becoming a freelancer illustrator in 1991 and founding Togoru Co., Ltd. with her husband in 2000. In 2017 the company was reborn as Togoru Art Works. She works with a wide range of genres including cover art and design for science fiction, mysteries and horror titles, as well as illustrations for children's books.
www.youchan.com

CPSIA information can be obtained
at www.ICGtesting.com
Printed in the USA
BVHW031104031019
560136BV00002B/445/P

9 784908 793127